Our National Holidays

by Patricia J. Murphy

Content Adviser: Kathleen M. Kendrick, Project Historian,
National Museum of American History, Smithsonian Institution

Social Science Adviser: Professor Sherry L. Field,
Department of Curriculum and Instruction,
College of Education, The University of Texas at Austin

Reading Adviser: Dr. Linda D. Labbo, Department of Reading Education,
College of Education, The University of Georgia

Compass Point Books
Minneapolis, Minnesota

Compass Point Books
3722 West 50th Street, #115
Minneapolis, MN 55410

Visit Compass Point Books on the Internet at *www.compasspointbooks.com* or e-mail your
request to *custserv@compasspointbooks.com*

Photographs ©: Reuters/Pat Benic/Hulton Getty/Archive Photos, cover; Robert Ginn/Photophile, 4; North Wind
Picture Archives, 6, 16; American Stock/Hulton Getty/Archive Photos, 8, 20; Stock Montage, 10; Reuters/Win
McNamee/Hulton Getty/Archive Photos 12; Corbis, 14; Unicorn Stock Photos/Joel Dexter, 18.

Editors: E. Russell Primm, Emily J. Dolbear, and Laura Driscoll
Photo Researchers: Svetlana Zhurkina and Jo Miller
Photo Selector: Linda S. Koutris
Designer: Melissa Voda

Library of Congress Cataloging-in-Publication Data
Murphy, Patricia J., 1963-
    Our national holidays / by Patricia J. Murphy.
      p. cm. — (Let's see library)
    Includes bibliographical references and index.
    Summary: Explains the reasons for various national patriotic holidays.
    ISBN 0-7565-0194-6
    1. Holidays—United States—Juvenile literature. [1. Holidays.] I. Title. II. Let's see library. Our nation.
 GT4803 .M87 2002
    394.26973—dc21   2001004484

Table of Contents

What Are National Holidays?

On national holidays, Americans **celebrate** their history. On these days, we may remember an important person or group of people. Or we may remember an important event in the country's history. The United States has many national holidays during the year.

Many businesses and government offices are closed on national holidays. You may have the day off from school. To celebrate, you may gather with your family. You may wave a flag or watch a parade.

◄ *On national holidays, you may wave a flag.*

What Was Our Country's First National Holiday?

The first national holiday in the United States was **Independence** Day. This is our country's birthday.

Before the 1770s, Britain ruled America. On July 4, 1776, a group of Americans finished writing the Declaration of Independence. This important paper said that America did not want Britain to rule it anymore.

Americans celebrated the first Independence Day on July 4, 1777. They lit candles, shot off fireworks, sang songs, and marched in parades.

◄ *In 1876, people in Philadelphia, Pennsylvania, celebrated America's 100th birthday with colorful parades.*

What Is Martin Luther King Jr. Day?

Dr. Martin Luther King Jr. was a great leader. He was born on January 15, 1929. He lived at a time when many laws treated African-Americans unfairly.

In the 1950s and 1960s, Dr. King worked hard to change this. He believed all people had the same rights. Some people did not agree. In 1968, someone shot and killed Dr. King.

Because of Dr. King and others, many unfair laws were changed. Americans celebrate the birthday of this leader on the third Monday in January. On this day, we remember what Dr. King did to make the world a better place.

◄ *Each January, we remember Dr. Martin Luther King Jr.*

What Is Presidents' Day?

On Presidents' Day, we honor George Washington, Abraham Lincoln, and all the other U.S. presidents. At one time, George Washington's birthday was celebrated on February 22. Abraham Lincoln's birthday was celebrated on February 12.

In 1971, President Richard Nixon turned the two holidays into one. He did this to honor all the presidents of the United States. Today, we celebrate Presidents' Day on the third Monday in February.

◄ *Presidents' Day honors George Washington and all the other U.S. presidents.*

What Is Memorial Day?

On Memorial Day, we remember American soldiers who died in battle. Memorial Day was first celebrated in 1868. It was called **Decoration** Day. People remembered soldiers who had died in the Civil War (1861–1865) by putting flowers and flags on their graves.

In 1882, the name was changed to Memorial Day. It was a day to remember Americans who died serving in any war.

Today, Memorial Day is celebrated on the last Monday in May. People remember soldiers as well as friends and family members who have died.

◀ *On Memorial Day, a soldier places a flag on a grave in Arlington National Cemetery in Washington, D.C.*

What Is Labor Day?

Labor Day is a holiday for workers. In fact, labor means "work." This holiday is celebrated on the first Monday in September.

The first Labor Day was held in 1882. American workers felt they had built a great country. They wanted a holiday to honor their hard work.

On the first Labor Day, there was a big parade in New York City. After the parade, many people enjoyed picnics. Millions of Americans celebrate Labor Day the same way today.

◄ *This 1908 photograph shows a Labor Day parade in Red Granite, Wisconsin.*

What Is Columbus Day?

Columbus Day is named for the Italian **explorer** Christopher Columbus. In 1492, Columbus sailed west from Europe. He wasn't sure what was on the other side of the Atlantic Ocean. In October, he landed in the Bahamas. There were people living there. Columbus called them Indians. He thought he had sailed around the world to Asia, which was known as the Indies. But he was in North America!

We celebrate Columbus Day on the second Monday in October. We may go to parades. We also may think about how Columbus's trip changed the lives of Native Americans.

◄ *Christopher Columbus's ships reached North America in October 1492.*

What Is Veterans Day?

Veterans Day is like a thank-you card from America to its armed forces. Many **veterans** risked their lives for our country.

Some Americans mark the day with a minute of silence at 11 A.M. Why? At 11 A.M. on November 11, 1918, World War I (1914–1918) ended. On November 11, 1919, the first Armistice Day honored veterans of this war.

In 1954, Armistice Day became Veterans Day. It became a day to honor all U.S. veterans. Today, we celebrate this holiday on the second Monday in November.

◀ *U.S. veterans celebrate Veterans Day.*

What Is Thanksgiving?

Many people say the first Thanksgiving was in 1621. That's when the first English settlers in Massachusetts invited the Indians to a big feast. Their crops were very good, and they wanted to celebrate. But it wasn't truly the first Thanks-giving. Native Americans and settlers had similar feasts in other colonies before 1621.

Today, we celebrate Thanksgiving Day on the fourth Thursday in November. Many celebrate the holiday by sharing a big meal with family and friends. It is a day to be thankful for what we have.

◀ *Pilgrims and Native Americans shared Thanksgiving dinner in 1621.*

Glossary

celebrate—to do something enjoyable to mark a special day

decoration—a badge or medal given as an honor

explorer—someone who searches for new places or new things

independence—freedom

veterans—people who have served in the armed forces, especially during a war

Did You Know?

• The word *holiday* comes from an old English word that means "holy day."

• The only holiday celebrated around the world is New Year's Day, on January 1.

• Each state decides which national holidays it will celebrate. The president and Congress designate which holidays Washington, D.C., and national employees will celebrate. These holidays usually fall on Mondays to give workers three-day weekends.

Want to Know More?

At the Library

Anderson, Joan. *The First Thanksgiving Feast*. New York: Clarion Books, 1989.
Penner, Lucille. Celebration: *The Story of American Holidays*. New York: Macmillan, 1993.
Spies, Karen. *Our National Holidays*. Brookfield, Conn.: Millbrook Press, 1994.

On the Web

Kid's Domain: Holidays
http://www.kidsdomain.com/holiday
For information on other national holidays and fun activities

United States Embassy, Stockholm, Sweden: Holidays in the U.S.A.
http://www.usemb.se/Holidays/celebrate/
For more detailed histories about each holiday

Through the Mail

Plimoth Plantation
P.O. Box 1620
Plymouth, MA 02362
To get specific information about the history of Thanksgiving

On the Road

Independence National Historical Park
313 Walnut Street
Philadelphia, PA 19106
215/597-8974
To see the Declaration of Independence and learn more about the birth of the nation celebrated on Independence Day

Index

About the Author
Patricia J. Murphy writes children's storybooks, nonfiction books,
early readers, and poetry. She also writes for magazines, corporations,
educational publishing companies, and museums. She is the owner of
PattyCake Productions and lives in Northbrook, Illinois.